For Barry, Maisie & J.J.

Thanks to my amazing other half Barry, for without his keen eye for detail and technical know how, my book would not be what it is. Thank you also to my Mum, my 'sisters' Elaine, Irene and Katrina for all their support, love and laughter.
Thanks to Robert & Gail, Paul & Michelle and Rab & Jan for always being there for us.

Kitty Kat Publishing LTD
Blue House Square
272 Bath Street
Glasgow   G2 4JR

Published 2012
ISBN 978 0 9574326 0 4

Kitty Cat Publishing LTD is a

D1514480

Scarlet Underpants

Meets the Tooth Fairy

Written by
Catherine Muir

Illustrated by
Sevilay Akçay

One day a girl, not too little but not too big either, was sitting in her house. She was very sad because some other children had been horrible to her about her name.

She was called Scarlet Underpants.
She had an older sister called Maisie Daisie and a younger brother called J.J.

Scarlet was in her sitting room when her daddy walked in.
"Hey up Scarlet are you all right?" he asked her with a loving warmth that only her daddy could bring.
"No Daddy I'm not!" she said indignantly. "Why do I have this silly, silly name! I hate it!"
Daddy asked, "What's wrong with the name Scarlet?"
"It's not Scarlet I don't like Daddy, it's UNDERPANTS!!
Why can't I have a normal name for goodness sake?"

Daddy said, "Scarlet sweetheart, you should be very proud of your name because your great, great, great, great, great, great, great, great, great, great, great, great, great, great, great, great grandfather and your great, great, great, great, great, great, great, great, great, great, great, great, great, great, great, great grandmother made the finest underpants in the whole world."

"People wanted to buy them in Africa, in India, America and China, Japan, Australia and Austria. In fact anywhere you can think of where there are people, they wanted to buy our underpants.
That was how we got our name.
Because we made the best underpants in the whole wide world."

If only they made chocolate or marshmallows or ice-lollys, she thought.

Scarlet contemplated what her name would be like then.

Scarlet Chocolate, she thought. Hmm, she did not like that any better.
She decided she was hungry and that was why she was thinking up names of sweet things, so she thought she would go and get something to eat.

In the kitchen her mummy and baby brother were sitting with some grapes and apples.
Scarlet tried to sneak into the fridge to get out something she knew Mummy would not want her to have this close to dinner.

Mummy said, "Scarlet, darling do you want to join us for some fruit?"
"Em, well, I'm not really hungry for fruit Mummy, I just wanted something sweet."
"Darling, dinner is almost ready. Why not just have a few grapes?"

Scarlet pulled a face as if Mummy had **actually** asked her to eat the contents of her baby brother's potty!

"I just wanted a sweet, not fruit," and with that she huffed out of the kitchen and into the back garden.

She was very lucky in the fact she had a big garden and her daddy built her a tree house.

Not just for her specifically, but for her and her brother and sister.

Although her brother had not actually been there when the tree house was built,

Daddy said that was a technicality and it was to be shared with him too.

Scarlet spent a lot of time in the tree house. It was her favourite place almost in the whole world.

Maisie Daisie didn't come up very often. She always had lots of friends to play with and was very good at everything she did.

No-one ever teased her about her name.

Scarlet was still in a huff inside the tree house when she thought she heard a noise.
She thought she heard her name.
She looked round very quickly and saw a snail on the floor of the tree house and said,
 "did you say my name?"

She listened carefully and could not believe her ears but she heard,
"Don't be so silly!!"

Scarlet looked round to where the voice had came from and she saw a great big bee.

"Was it you who spoke to me?" She looked very puzzled.

"Don't be silly," said the voice again.

Scarlet looked round again and saw a cat just outside the tree house.

She just pointed and said....

"No!"

"Me of course, silly girl!"

As Scarlet turned around she saw a very pretty tiny girl with

sparkly almost see through wings.

"Who are you?" Scarlet said, a bit dazed almost as if she were dreaming.

"I'm Penny Moneytree. I'm a fairy."

"What …?" was all that Scarlet was able to stammer.

"I heard you talking earlier to your Dad about your name. I thought that was a shame and I should come and introduce myself to you.

After all we are # neighbours.

"What do you mean neighbours?"
"Well," said Penny Moneytree, "I live here."
"Where?"

"In this house of course."

"Are you telling me that you are a fairy who lives in my tree house?"

"Yes of course," said the fairy.

"I thought fairies lived under toadstools?"
Scarlet managed to say.
"Well some do but I like a bit of space,"
the fairy answered.

"Anyway," said the fairy sounding very much like Scarlet's mummy, "my name is Penny Moneytree.
I say this name with pride because my family grows the money trees for the tooth fairies.
It's a very special skill too. If the trees were not looked after properly, they would eventually die and tooth fairies would run out of money to give to the children.
"That would be terrible," said Scarlet.

"The smaller the tree is, the less money grows on it.
That's why different children get different amounts of money per tooth.
It's just luck really who you get as your fairy and what tree they have been

assigned to."

"I always wondered about that," said Scarlet really interested now and not feeling strange anymore.

"So, what do you do with all the teeth you take then?" asked Scarlet,

because this was something else she always wanted to know.

"We plant them at the bottom of the money tree of course. It's the magic from the children's teeth that makes the trees grow."

"Ohh, I see!" said Scarlet.

"Thank you for telling me that."

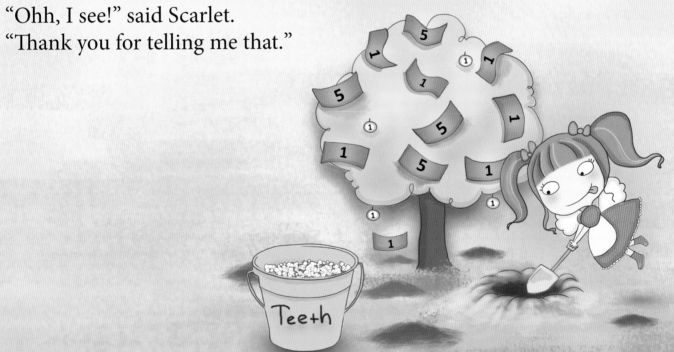

"Does anyone ever make fun of you because of your name?"

"I don't really know," said Penny Moneytree and she continued, "I am very proud of my name as you should be of yours.

Our name is what links us to people who lived before us. It's what they were."

"If some silly fairy were to tease me I would simply

ignore them or tell them how silly they are or

perhaps both.

If people are not nice to you, you should feel sorry for them, not yourself, because they are missing out on the chance to be friends with someone truly wonderful."

"Thanks," said Scarlet.
"That makes me feel a lot better."

"You're welcome Scarlet.

Anyway, real friends are nice to you, like my friend Rarajaja. He's a dragon. Would you like to meet him? He's coming for dinner tomorrow."

"A real live dragon, I thought they were fierce and

dangerous and breathe fire and eat children!"
said Scarlet.

"Have you met any dragons?"
"No."
"So how do you
know what they
are like?"

"I don't I suppose I do, but I have heard bad things about them."
"That's silly to judge someone before you meet them," said Penny
Moneytree.
"And that was just a rumour that the elves made up because they fell out
with the dragons."

Just then there was a very odd noise, it sounded almost like a snuffly, barking, meowing, tweeting kind of noise.

"What's that?" asked Scarlet.

"That's my communication device." She picked up this strange looking thing, shaped a bit like a rock and a snake and a cake.

"Hi, yes it is Penny Moneytree.
Oh hi, I didn't recognise your voice there. I was just talking about you. Can you still come for dinner?

Fantastic!

You can meet my new friend, **Scarlet Underpants**. Yes! I know, it's a fantastic name.
See you then. Bye.

Will you come and meet him tomorrow ?"
"That would be lovely...... I think?" said Scarlet, still a bit scared.

Hello Penny!

the top spins

flashing cherry

like a cake

press buttons
to communicate

pictures of friends
(.. fairy, dragon, frog and more ..)

like a snake

this bit spins

this bit stays still

like a rock

hold at the bottom

same size as a grapefruit

"See you tomorrow then," said Penny Moneytree shuffling Scarlet out the door of the treehouse, "I hear your Mum calling you for dinner."

"Okay Mum, I'm on my way."
Scarlet turned to say goodbye to Penny Moneytree but she was nowhere to be seen.
"Goodbye Penny Moneytree and thanks. I'll see you tomorrow."

Scarlet went into the house and **kissed** her mum and dad, her sister and hugged her baby brother. She felt fantastic now about her name and her family and of a long time ago when they made the best underpants the world had ever known.

The Finest Underpants
In The Whole World

Catherine Muir is a dedicated Mum of two who has worked in children's television for many years.

Having taken some time out to spend with her children, she found some interesting ways to entertain them.

This book is based on a character that developed over the years of nursing illnesses, dealing with the everyday problems of growing up and telling stories when kids sometimes need a little subtle guidance.